So What!

There are 12 brilliant titles in the **Kitty and friends** series.

Collect them all!

I don't want to!

I can't find it!

It's not fair!

But you promised!

Why not?

I know!

I'm scared!

I wish!

Why me?

I'm bored!

It's not my fault!

So what!

Bel Mooney

illustrated by Margaret Chamberlain

EGMONT

First published in Great Britain 2002
by Egmont Books Limited,
239 Kensington High Street, London W8 6SA

ISBN 0 7497 4823 0

3 5 7 9 10 8 6 4

A CIP catalogue record for this title
is available from the British Library

Printed in Great Britain
by Cox & Wyman Ltd, Reading, Berkshire

Contents

For
James, Imogen
and Clement Faux

A Letter from **Kitty**

Hi Everyone!

Shall I let you into a **secret?** Sometimes I think I **don't ever want** to grow up. Do you feel that way? But we can't stop it **happening, can we?**

In this **book my** baby brother has a birthday and I don't like all the **fuss that's** made over him. Lots of **other** things happen **which** I don't

like much either, but **sometimes I think** you **have** to shrug your **shoulders, pretend you** don't care, and say, 'So what!' **Of course,** usually you **do care**

MUM, TOM AND DANIEL

- very much.

The point is, as you get a little bit older, GUs (like my mum and dad!) expect you to act a little bit older too. But you **can't** always manage that, can you? Anyway - I can't. Isn't life **complicated** sometimes?

Now, I've got something to tell you. This is the **twelfth** and last in the series of stories about me and my family. I hope you **collect** them all.

But there will be all sorts of fun books about me and my **friends** coming **soon**, so make sure you look out for **those**.

→ DAD

You can visit Bel's website (**www.bel-mooney.co.uk**) and read all about the Kitty books, and leave messages saying what you think about me and my adventures, and maybe even suggest what Bel ought to write next. She'd like that, and so would I.

MR TUBBS

That's all for now!

Love

Kitty

chapter 1
Homework!

Mum was always calling Kitty lazy. Kitty didn't like that at all.

'Look, Mum,' she yelled, 'I was rushing around all morning with William, and this afternoon Rosie and I played football and tonight I beat Daniel at draughts for once and then we had to watch TV and that cartoon serial was so scary it made me run and hide behind the armchair, and . . . Phew, I'm really tired! How can you call me lazy?'

'You haven't tidied your room and – far more important – you haven't done your homework,' Mum said.

'Oh *that*!' said Kitty.

On Sunday morning Kitty slept and slept, although she did imagine some dream person kept calling her and telling her to get up.

At last Mum swooped on her and pulled back the duvet.

'Up!' she commanded.

'It's too early,' Kitty moaned.

'It's halfway through the day. You're just being lazy!' said Mum.

'Oh – so what?' Kitty mumbled into her pillow.

'*What* did you say?' asked Mum, sounding a bit frightening.

'Nothing!' said Kitty innocently, swinging her legs to the floor.

The day was full of things to do. Kitty

ducked through the gap in the fence into William's garden to meet him. They spent a long time seeing who could throw a little garden fork the furthest, so that it stuck in the grass with its handle in the air. They argued over who should pace out the distances, but in the end William won.

After that they played for a while with William's new black and white kitten, Cleo, who loved chasing pieces of string round and round. At last William and Kitty were out of breath, although Cleo could have gone on for hours.

Dad called Kitty in for pasta, and she had to use a lot of energy between every mouthful telling him how good it was, because cooking was his new hobby and he liked them all to make a fuss. Mum fed baby Tom. Daniel complained at having to sit at the table because he wanted to take his plate to watch TV, but Dad didn't allow that.

'Not when I've gone to the trouble to make a nice meal,' he said firmly.

'So what?' muttered Daniel. 'I'd rather have beans on toast.'

'Typical!' said Dad, sounding half-cross and half-hurt.

'*I* love it, Dad, and *I* think it's better to eat *good* food,' said Kitty sweetly, because she liked it when Mum and Dad were cross with Daniel.

So what!

The afternoon went very quickly. Kitty knew she was supposed to write down some ideas for a story and a picture, both inspired by one of her favourite books. Next week was Book Week and a famous author called Margie Grey was coming on Monday to take their class and help them with their story ideas. Kitty was very excited because she liked this writer's books very much. But even so, she decided that tidying was better than homework.

The truth is, Kitty used to like drawing pictures and writing stories, but now – sometimes – she couldn't really be bothered. It felt too much like hard work. So when they were given homework she did everything to avoid doing it, whatever the subject was.

Kitty wanted to please Mum by making her room look a bit better. There were clothes all over the place, and a pile of books on the floor, and all her felt-tips were scattered where she'd knocked them off her little table.

She moved the books to the table, one by one, listening to her radio, and stopping for a while to dance to her favourite song. It took a long time to collect the felt-tips and when she'd got them all together, another song she liked came on, so she chucked them on the bed and did another dance.

It was so boring picking up clothes, because some of them were clean and some dirty and it wasn't always easy to see which was which. So Kitty collected them all together and dumped them on her bed, but then they covered up the felt-tips, which really she needed if she was going to do her homework.

It was all so tiring!

On Saturday morning she'd laid out her new exercise book, with a lovely picture of two dolphins on the front, intending to write down story ideas. But Saturday had gone and so had half of Sunday, and now the pile of books she'd put on the table fell over on top of it – some of them toppling back on the floor.

The room looked worse than ever. Kitty didn't think it mattered one bit if you lived in what Mum called a 'tip', but Mum said it mattered a lot, and GUs always believe they're right. So if she asked 'Who cares?', as she often did these days, Mum always snapped, '*I* care – and that's enough!'

You couldn't win.

When she went downstairs for tea Mum was fussing over the baby as usual, but looked up and asked if Kitty had done all her jobs.

'I tidied my room – sort of,' said Kitty.

'And your homework?'

Kitty hesitated before she said, 'I did that too.'

So what!

★ ★ ★

Next morning William's sister Sally walked along with them, before going on to her big school. William asked Kitty if she'd written down a story idea. 'No, I didn't have time,' she said.

'Oh, Kit – but Margie Grey's coming,' he said.

'So what?' she said airily.

'Well, you won't know what to say,' he replied.

'Huh! Like I said – so what? I'll just make it up as I go along,' she laughed.

'That's right, Kit, homework's a waste of time,' said Sally. 'Wait till you get to our school. You'll be squashed by it every day.'

She pretended to walk along bent double under an invisible heavy load, and she looked so funny William and Kitty giggled, and Kitty thought no more about the homework she hadn't done.

When Margie Grey walked into the

classroom Kitty felt so excited she could hardly breathe. A real writer! She looked wonderful, with short dark hair, lots of rings and bracelets, high-heeled boots and a big purple shawl. There was the lady who'd written all those great stories, and she'd come to talk to *them*!

Margie Grey began by talking to them about her own stories, and how sometimes she had brilliant ideas when she was gazing out of the window.

Yes – and Mum calls that day-dreaming, thought Kitty. Just wait till I tell her!

Then Kitty's favourite writer said she was looking forward to hearing all their story ideas. The children had their notebooks out and looked eager. One or two started to stretch their hands high because they wanted to be chosen. But Kitty's dolphin book remained closed on the table.

'I think I'll just point at people in turn, because I don't know your names,' Margie smiled. 'Now – let me see – what about you over there?'

Oh no, Kitty thought, it can't be . . .

'Yes, the little girl with the longish dark hair and the blue and black striped jumper – you – that's right! You start by reading me what you've written.'

Kitty wanted the ground to open and

swallow her up. Usually she was full of ideas – and words too. But now there was a big blank space shining in her skull, so brightly it made her blink.

'Go *on*, Kitty,' hissed their teacher, looking worried. She wanted their famous visitor to be pleased.

Kitty felt her mouth gape like a fish. She glanced down at her closed exercise book, and wished – *so much* – she'd done some preparation. Oh, what ever can I say? she thought desperately. She felt so silly.

On the cover, plunging through the waves, the big dolphin and the little one looked so carefree. But that look in the eye of the smaller dolphin – wasn't it a bit naughty?

Inspiration!

'My story will be about a mummy dolphin and a baby dolphin, and the baby dolphin doesn't listen to her mum, so nearly gets caught by the big nets, but it all ends happily,' she said, 'and I got the idea from that story you wrote about the rabbits, when the baby one runs away and nearly gets eaten by the fox.'

'Very good – er – Kitty. Now, ideas like that are for stories that teach us something about ourselves, aren't they? But sometimes stories can just be for fun. Who's got a funny story idea for me? Yes – *you*!'

She pointed to Rosie, and soon everybody was laughing. The whole lesson passed very quickly. All the children were really keen, and having a proper author there to help them with their thoughts made them all feel like real writers themselves.

When the bell rang they all applauded Margie Grey and she told them to keep reading good books and to keep writing too. 'All of you here have a whole pile of stories inside you. What you have to do is open the door and let them out! Goodbye now.'

'Wasn't she lovely?' said Rosie.

'She was so pretty,' sighed Anita.

'I liked her earrings,' said Kitty.

'Hey, Kit, you were lucky to be able to think up that stuff about the dolphins so quickly,' said William, and explained to the others that Kitty hadn't done her homework.

'Why?' Rosie asked. 'Usually you love stories and stuff like that. It's me who doesn't!'

'I didn't have the time,' Kitty protested.

'Too lazy to bother, more like it,' laughed William.

'So what?' Kitty shrugged.

Then as she linked arms with Rosie and Anita she added, 'Hey, I still think homework's a bit of a waste of time. But I'll do it next time – not 'cos I'm good but 'cos it's much too much like hard work to make up ideas on the spot like I did.

Mum's right – I'm too lazy!'

chapter 2
The wood's vanished!

On the edge of the town where Kitty lived there were the usual roads and roundabouts, and a big supermarket. Sometimes she saw all the cars and lorries and wondered where everybody could possibly be going.

But there were some woods and fields too, and when she and Daniel were little Mum and Dad would often take them out to the country for a walk. There was one place she particularly liked, where they'd had fun. It was a small wood full of whispering trees, but they hadn't visited it for a very, very long time.

One day in spring Kitty had Anita over to spend the day with her, and after a while they felt bored. They had run out of things to do and William was out visiting relatives.

Then Kitty had a brainwave. The sun was shining and Mum and Dad seemed relaxed and Baby Tom wasn't crying as much as usual, so Kitty announced her plan.

'Why don't we go on a family outing this afternoon?'

'Yes, I could do with some fresh air,' Dad said.

'But where?' said Mum.

'Can we take some food?' asked Daniel.

'Fa-fa-fa-gagaga,' said Baby Tom.

'It's not far,' Kitty said, 'but do you

remember that little wood where we went and the last time you and I found a sort of den where two trees had grown together?'

Daniel did remember and his face lit up. 'That must have been two years ago, and I was more of a kid then. But I'd still like to see it again.'

'So would I. Hey, Anita, you'll love it. It's a sort of special, magic place,' Kitty said.

'That's decided then,' smiled Mum.

It didn't take them long to get ready, and soon they were bowling along, Mum

and Dad in the front of the car, and Anita, Kitty and Dan squashed around Tom's baby seat. It was such a lovely day, they all felt very happy.

But when they reached the place Kitty remembered they were shocked.

'Oh dear,' said Mum.

'The wood's vanished!' cried Kitty.

'You couldn't have made a den here,' whispered Anita.

'Dad! You must have gone the wrong way,' Daniel complained.

'Uk! Uk!' went Tom, pointing as if he'd seen something very exciting.

They got out of the car and walked across to a spot that wasn't special or magical at all. Not any more.

It was like a scene from a war movie. There was a big high fence around the wood, with a huge sign saying, ROCKFACE DEVELOPMENTS. A few of the trees were still standing, but most were lying broken on the ground. The soil was churned up, and there were vast holes where the trees' roots had been.

Over on the far side a bulldozer was busy: backwards and forwards it went, pushing, pushing at a chestnut tree until it had no chance. It crashed over with a sort of screaming sound. All the leaves trembled as it lay there on the ground.

'What a mess!' shouted Kitty.

'Sorry, kids, not much of an outing,' said Mum sadly.

'What are they doing?' asked Daniel.

Dad said he had completely forgotten reading in the local paper that after a lot of protests and petitions the developers had finally got the go ahead to build a business park.

'What's a business park?' Anita asked.

She was holding Kitty's hand because she could see her friend was upset.

'Oh, there'll be lots of small buildings where local firms have offices. I think I read there'll be a furniture workshop as well,' Dad said. 'The thing is, it's very good for making jobs for people – do you see that?'

Daniel nodded, but Kitty shook her head furiously. 'So what?' she yelled.

They walked back to the car, but Kitty didn't want to go, even though the sight of what was left of the wood and the memory of their den made her sad.

'I hate it,' she cried, stamping her foot in rage. 'What about all those lovely trees?'

'Poor trees,' sighed Anita.

Daniel liked to annoy Kitty, and now he pretended to be very hard. 'Come on, Kit – so what's it matter if a few old trees are cut down? You've got to have progress! Dad says there'll be lots of jobs for people, and I think people are more important than trees, so there!'

'But what about the birds? What about all the mice and voles and hedgehogs and moles, and all the other little animals who lived there? Yes! And what about the billions and zillions of insects and tiny little things who lived in the bark? Where've they all gone?' Kitty replied. She wanted to cry.

'Oh, they'll have found new places to live,' said Daniel carelessly.

'Not so easy, 'cos the town's spreading outwards,' Mum said, looking a bit sad as she clutched Baby Tom. 'I worry about it too, Kitty. I don't want Tom – or any of you – to grow up in a world that's all concrete. There's got to be more to life than making money!'

'You wouldn't like it, Dan! You wouldn't like some great big bulldozer to come along and push our house over, so we had to run away!' said Kitty.

Dan didn't say anything, because he knew that was true. They all got in the car, feeling that the spring sun had disappeared – even though in fact it still hung in the sky like a great big tennis ball.

On the way home they were all quiet, but then Dad seemed to be going the wrong way, so Mum asked what he was doing.

'It's a surprise,' he said.

They reached the town centre and Dad

told Mum to take Kitty, Daniel and Baby Tom for ice-creams.

'Anita – you can come and help me,' he said.

Anita, who was very shy, seemed to grow a lot taller at that – she was so pleased Kitty's dad had chosen her. She grinned and felt important.

When they all met at the car again about thirty minutes later, Anita's smile was even wider.

'What have you bought?' Kitty asked suspiciously.

'It's in the boot!' Anita crowed, jumping up and down.

When they got home Dad opened the back of the car, winked at Anita, and took out a large cardboard box. He held it high, so Kitty couldn't possibly see what was inside, and carried it into the house.

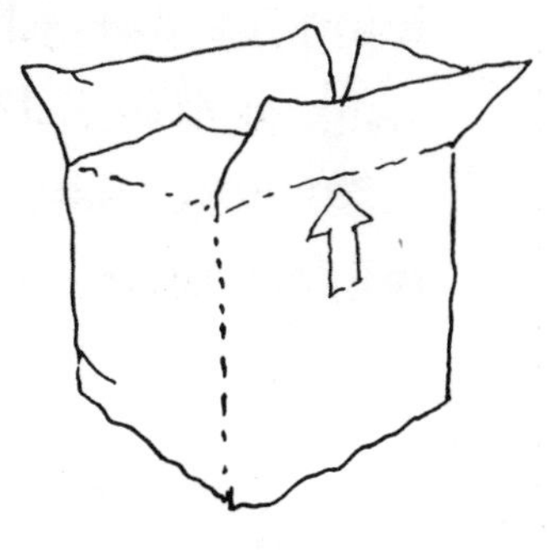

'I'm just as curious as

you, Kitty-Kat,' smiled Mum.

Tom said, 'Ka-ka-ka-ka-ka.'

Dad didn't stop in the hall, or the living room, or the kitchen. He balanced the box, unlocked the back door, and marched straight out into the garden. Then he put the box down on the little paved area he'd built last year and said, 'I paid a visit to that great new pet and wildlife centre. There you are, gang! You can unpack it all.'

They crowded round. Kitty couldn't believe it. There were two nesting boxes, one to fix high in the trees at the bottom of the garden, and another one for the top of the garden shed. Dad had also bought two little nesting pockets made of reeds, which looked very cosy, and a strange little hanging hut which he explained was a 'bug house'. Then Anita held up two hedgehog boxes – little curved homes with tiny entrances.

'I chose those!' she cried.

Dad explained, 'If you put them in the bushes hedgehogs will come because they always need somewhere safe to stay.'

Last of all, there was a proper wooden bird table, with a little roof so it looked like a park shelter. Dad promised he'd get out his hammer and nails and make a long pole for it to sit on top of, so Cleo the kitten couldn't attack the birds.

'So – you bought lots of little homes!' Kitty cried, her eyes shining.

'Yes love, and although I can't say that some of the creatures from the woodland will come all the way here, at least we can make our garden a little haven for some other ones, can't we?' said Dad gently.

Kitty wanted to cry again, but for a different reason this time.

Mum said Dad was brilliant, and Baby Tom clapped his hands, and Anita looked so happy that she'd been a part of

the secret.

Daniel said nothing. He looked almost sulky, as if he felt left out. But Kitty knew it was because he felt he'd said the wrong thing and felt a bit bad.

Dad saw that too. He put an arm round his son. 'The thing is, Dan,' he said gently, 'there's all sorts of complicated reasons

when a road or a supermarket or a factory gets built, making us lose another bit of the countryside. All I want you to think is this – it *does* matter. It *always* matters. OK?'

Daniel looked at Kitty.

She waited.

He nodded and said, 'OK . . . Now, Kit – let's get these little houses sorted out!'

chapter 3
Big bully!

There was a new boy in their class. He was called Tim, and Kitty wasn't sure she liked him. Tim had very short cropped hair, and was taller than any of the others, even Rosie. He didn't say much, but what he didn't say was rather scary!

Tim walked around with his shoulders square and his nose in the air – as if he couldn't be bothered talking to little squirts like them. He hung around with Jason and one or two of the others, but even those big boys were a bit in awe of him because they soon discovered he was a real football star. But he could be a bit rough when he played, so some of the boys started calling him 'Tough Tim' and the name stuck.

Even when Tim had been at the school for about three weeks Kitty felt that nobody really knew him. Sometimes she wondered if he lived in a world of his own because he liked it – or because secretly he was afraid nobody liked him. These days she often asked herself questions like that about people.

One day Kitty noticed William was rather quiet. As the days passed he seemed to become more and more silent, as if there was a padlock weighing down the corners of his mouth.

'What's up, William?' she asked, when he was at her house.

'Nothing,' he shrugged.

'Yes there is.'

'No there isn't.'

'Come on! You and I have been friends since we were one! Don't tell me fibs.'

So what!

'I told you, Kitty, nothing's wrong! Why don't you stop poking your nose in!'

With that, William slammed the door and rushed back to his own house without saying goodbye. For a few moments Kitty was shocked and hurt. Then she realised something must be wrong.

She decided to keep an eye on William. She'd be a spy trying to find out secrets to save the life of a dear friend threatened by some terrible danger.

In school Kitty watched William as much as she could without him knowing. Sometimes she wished she had eyes like a fly, that could see in all directions at once! 'I'd look a bit funny if I did!' she laughed to herself.

Of course, one place she couldn't follow William into was the boys' toilets. But at break time, when she saw him come out, she thought he looked very red and upset. I wonder why? she thought.

Rather than follow William she decided to wait and see who came out after him. It wasn't long before Tim sauntered out, hands in his pockets and that strange, closed-off look on his face. He didn't notice Kitty, who now decided something was badly wrong.

Next day she saw Tim walk past William and roughly push a note into his pocket. That's very odd, she thought.

But it was when she was watching the boys play football that Kitty guessed the truth. William was her oldest friend, and she knew two things about him. He wasn't very good at football and he wished – oh so much! – that he was. So he tried very hard, and sometimes he looked a teeny bit funny – more like a puppet than a footballer.

Tim, on the other hand, was like the starriest player in the country, and he certainly looked the part, with his short hair! He could tackle and dribble like a dream, and when Kitty saw him race up the wing it was like watching a rocket being launched. He was brilliant – and she noticed how he lost his sullen look.

But she saw something else too. There was one time when William was free and he shouted to Tim, who had the ball as usual, to pass it to him. He looked so keen and eager. But Tim ignored him completely. He didn't even give him a chance. Just by dancing past as if the ball was glued to his right foot, Tim made William look really silly.

Not long after that, to Kitty's horror, Tim deliberately cannoned into William with his shoulder and sent him flying.

William lay in the mud and all the other boys laughed. The games teacher didn't seem to see.

No wonder they say all referees are blind, Kitty thought angrily.

'So that's it!' she said aloud, as she walked away. She felt so angry she wanted to rush on to that pitch and pummel Tim with her fists, no matter how tall he was.

When she and William were walking home, a few paces behind William's mum, who was chatting away to a friend, Kitty found the moment to speak.

'William,' she said, 'I know what's been going on. It's no good denying it, 'cos I've seen it. For some reason Tim's been picking on you. I don't know *why* it's you . . .'

'He says I'm a wimp and a weed,' said William miserably.

'Oh Will, you've never been the world's toughest boy, and that's why everybody loves you. But the point is, what are you going to do about it?'

'Nothing.'

'Nothing?'

'He wrote me a note saying he'll make me sorry if I tell. The other day he said I had to give him 50p too.'

'I don't believe this!' Kitty said.

'I wish it wasn't true,' said William.

That night Kitty thought hard about William's problems. She remembered the time Anita was being bullied on the way home from school, and she'd come up with a plan to save her. But that was older children, and she'd got the help of Rosie's family – and so it was all a lot easier.

She didn't know what to do about Tim.

Or at least – she had one plan, but it made her very nervous.

Next day, when the bell went for break time, Kitty took William to one side. She told him she'd been thinking hard about his problem. He looked worried.

'The thing is, Kit – it's my problem, not yours,' he said.

'No – that's not true. If your friend's got a problem that *is* your problem,' she retorted, 'and you have to do something about it, if you possibly can.'

'Oh Kit – but what?'

'I'm going to tell Tim to leave you alone. I'm going to tell him picking on you just proves to the world he's a really *sad* person. I'm going to tell him what I think of him!'

'No you can't!' William gasped.

'Why?'

'Because he's much bigger than you!'

'So what?'

'He might . . . he might hit you, Kitty!'

'So what? That'll just *prove* to everybody how sad he is.'

With that, Kitty turned on her heels and went stomping off across the playground in search of Tough Tim. Hair flying, heart thumping, she walked past Rosie and Anita. Something about her attitude made everybody stare – and follow her, to see what was going on.

At last she found Tim, leaning against the wall, chewing gum. As usual he was on his own, looking sullen and threatening. Without giving herself time to think, Kitty planted herself in front of him, hands on hips.

'So here you are! I've got a bone to pick with you,' she shouted in her loudest voice.

'Did I hear a fly buzz?' he asked the empty air above her head.

'Why are you being so mean to my friend William?'

'Who's he?'

'Don't make me crosser than I already am, Tim,' she said, drawing herself up to her full height – which wasn't very high. 'William's the boy you've been bullying. And *he* didn't tell me. I've been watching you!'

'So what?' he sneered. 'Who cares?' He shrugged and started to stroll away.

But Kitty barred his way. 'No, you don't! And you might as well know – *I* care, Tim – and a lot of other people round here care too!'

The other children started to nod their heads. But Kitty took no notice of them. She felt this was just between her and Tim and she had to win the battle of words. What she didn't notice was that William had come up too, and was standing nearby with his hand up to his mouth.

Tim noticed him and jeered, 'Well now, look everybody, there's the big brave Billy-goat! What's it like being defended by your little girlfriend? Oh SAD!'

Kitty stood up straight, darted forward and jabbed Tim hard in the arm with fingers outstretched like an arrow. Taken by surprise, he jumped back.

'Listen!' she said, 'I may be a girl but I'm not afraid of you! Right now I think you're a bit afraid of me. And yes, I'm William's friend, but at least he's *got* people to stick up for him! You might think you're tough, but you're standing here on your own! You haven't made one friend! What's *really* sad is somebody who comes to a new school and doesn't even bother to fit in. Hey, everybody – isn't that pathetic?'

This time the other children chorused,

'Yes!' – and Tim went red. He stepped back, and Kitty moved even closer to him, wagging a finger.

'Listen, Tim, I'll do a deal with you, OK?'

'What deal?' he mumbled sulkily.

'It's Friday today, and you've got the weekend to decide to make a new start. On Monday you can be the New Tim. And if you are we'll give you a second chance, won't we, everyone?'

'Yes!' they cried. Tim looked from one to the other, then turned quickly and walked away.

Rosie, Anita and William crowded round Kitty, followed by the others. They patted her on the back, and said how brave she was.

But she shook her head.

'Tim may be big and tough, but so what? I think he's really small and lonely inside,' she said thoughtfully. 'That's why I think he will try to be better next week. Let's all help him, hey?'

And he did.

And so did they.

chapter 4
Cry baby!

'Hip hip hooray – Tom's one today!'

Daniel was just as excited as a toddler, Kitty thought crossly – going around singing that silly little song. Anybody would think a baby had never had a birthday before. 'Who's his mumma's little gwown up boysie, den?' crooned Mum in that voice that drove Kitty mad.

'Come here, funny little man,' cooed Dad, holding out his arms.

So what!

'Da-da-da-da-da,' babbled Baby Tom.

'See how he loves his daddy,' smiled Mum.

'Mummmm-mu-mu-mu,' Tom went.

'And his mummy, too,' sighed Dad, as if he was so happy he might burst.

Dad's eyes shone, and Mum's were wet. 'I can't believe she's getting weepy,' Kitty said to herself as she stomped out of the kitchen. 'Huh, all it takes is one silly little kid burbling away on his silly old birthday and GUs turn into cry babies.'

Kitty was jealous. She hadn't liked it one bit when Mum and Dad told her they were having a surprise baby, and she hadn't liked it much when he was born. Since then she'd just about got used to having him in the house.

Sometimes he made her laugh and she thought he was quite sweet, but it still annoyed her when Mum and Dad looked at his fat little face as if there was only one child in the whole universe, and that was Baby Tom.

She *hated* that.

Now she decided it was stupid of Mum and Dad to give him presents because after all, he was too young to know what a birthday means. She'd forgotten they gave her Mr Tubs on her first birthday. And she dreaded that afternoon, because as well as

So what!

Uncle Joe, Auntie Susan and Melissa, two of Mum's friends with babies were coming along for the grand birthday tea.

'Ooh good,' said Dan. 'There'll be lots of tasty stuff to eat. And a cake!'

'So what! It'll just be *boring*,' Kitty moaned, 'with everybody making a fuss over Tom.'

'All you want is for people to make a fuss over *you*,' snapped Daniel.

Kitty went to hit him, but he dodged her and ran away laughing. Kitty was chasing him, shouting, 'You come back here, I hate you!' when she bumped into Dad, who was carrying Tom down the hall.

'Be careful, Kitty! You might have knocked the baby out of my arms,' he shouted.

'Behave yourself, Kitty, I don't want any unpleasantness on Tom's big day,' said Mum sternly.

Not long after that Mum said she was going to take Tom out in his pushchair for a walk in the park. She asked Kitty if she wanted to come to play on the swings.

Kitty shook her head.

'Why love?'

'I just don't want to.'

'Please yourself,' said Mum, 'but you can help me by getting Tom into his coat while I go upstairs and put my trainers on.'

Tom was sitting on the living-room floor. Mum handed Kitty his little blue coat, then left the room. Kitty took one of his pudgy little arms and started to stuff it into the sleeve of the coat. Tom wriggled.

'Keep still, Tom!' she exclaimed.

It was quite hard getting the baby into his coat. When she used to dress up Mr Tubs it was easy to push his arms and legs around because, after all, he was only made of cloth and stuffing. But a real life baby with a mind of his own? That was quite different.

Kitty knew she was being a tiny bit quick and un-gentle in her actions, but she told herself that was because Mum would be downstairs any minute and she was in a rush.

'Owwwwwww!' yelled Tom suddenly.

'Shhhhhh,' hissed Kitty.

'Waaaaah waaaah!' he cried, louder and louder.

Mum came running in, wearing her trainers and fleece. 'What's the matter now? Why's he crying?'

'Cos he's a silly crybaby, Kitty thought, but said, 'I don't know, he probably didn't want his coat on, that's all.'

'Come here, my sweetheart . . . come to Mumma for a cuddle, my birthday boy,' murmured Mum, scooping the baby up in her arms and kissing him. 'Stop crying now . . . there . . . there. We don't want you crying, do we, eh? Shhhhh. Oh, Kitty, look at his little face . . .'

Kitty looked up resentfully.

'So what? Does it matter if he cries his head off?' she asked in a spiteful voice.

Mum looked down reproachfully. 'It matters, Kitty, because it means he's unhappy. And it's not very nice if *anyone*'s unhappy, is it?'

What about *me* then? Kitty thought, as she wandered out into the garden. *I'm* not very happy but nobody cares about *me*.

At four-thirty the birthday guests started to arrive. Mum had made little sandwiches, and laid out chocolate fingers, jaffa cakes, and put crisps in bowls. There were cubes of cheese and baby tomatoes, and lemonade or apple juice to drink. Dad gave Uncle Joe a beer, and Mum told her friends, Carol and Jan, that once they'd had a cup of tea they'd have to stay for a glass of white wine.

'We'll have to toast Tom properly,' she

beamed.

'Party time for Tom!' said Dad.

'He's the birthday baby!' grinned Dan.

Carol and Jan had babies about Tom's age. There was a lot of fuss and baby-talk, and the living room felt very crowded. Everybody gave him little packages, and he ripped the paper off and banged his

gifts around.

'Isn't Tom sweet!' said Melissa.

'If you like that sort of thing,' mumbled Kitty.

'Don't talk to Kitty, she's a grump,' said Daniel. Since their cousin had a new haircut and normal clothes instead of the party dresses she used to wear, Daniel liked her. He took Melissa off to get something to eat, and they stayed by the table chatting about their favourite TV programmes.

The GUs were all laughing and talking and eating. Mum was showing Tom the big new fire engine his aunt and uncle had brought, with big chunky firemen who sat along the top. To be honest, he seemed more interested in his baby visitors, Sam and Grace, who sat on the rug with him waving chocolate fingers about.

Soon all the babies had sticky faces, and the floor was covered in toys and paper, and Mum opened a bottle of white wine, and Dad put on a Beatles CD, and everybody seemed very happy.

Mum blew out the one candle on the birthday cake, because Tom didn't seem quite sure what he had to do, and they all sang 'Happy Birthday', while the three babies looked amazed at all the noise.

Then Dad said, 'Come on everybody, let's have a toast to Tom. Get yourself a glass of lemonade, Kitty, so you can join in!'

'I don't want any,' Kitty mumbled.

Dad glared at her, and Mum rolled her eyes, but they just carried on as if she hadn't spoken. Everybody shouted, 'Here's to Tom!' and raised their glasses, then cheered.

Kitty felt that everybody in the room was inside a beautiful, big, shining bubble, and she was on the outside looking in. She wanted them all to go away, so she wouldn't have to feel like this any more.

At last the party was over, and they did leave. There was a great noise of goodbyes by the front door, but Kitty stayed nibbling crisps on her own. Fuss, fuss, fuss, she thought.

Dad, Daniel and Mum did a quick tidy, then Mum took Baby Tom upstairs for his bath. Daniel had to rush because he was going to his friend's house to stay the night, and Dad was to drive him there. The living room suddenly seemed very quiet.

Kitty could hear Mum singing to Tom in the echoey bathroom. It sounded lovely. Kitty listlessly went on picking up wrapping paper as she'd promised, hearing the splashing and wishing it was the old days when she was little, and Mum would take her out of the bath, wrap her in a big fluffy towel, and cuddle her, whilst Kitty sucked her thumb.

Life was so much easier when you were very young, she thought.

Soon Mum came downstairs with Tom, who looked round, pink and shining in his new rabbit pyjamas.

'He's quite wide-awake now, so I want you to look after him for a bit, while I do the washing-up,' Mum said. 'I'll put some cartoons on, and you can sit on the settee with him, OK, love?'

Kitty grunted, and within seconds she was doing as Mum asked. To tell the truth, she liked the way Tom smelt when he was clean – of soap, shampoo and sweet-baby – and thought he looked very cuddly in his all-in-one outfit. So it was rather nice to loll there with her arm around him to keep him safe – and forget about the silly old birthday.

The trouble was, Kitty liked watching TV leaning on a cushion on the floor, closer to the screen than the sofa. So after a short time she got up.

'You stay there and don't move, Tom!' she said, wagging her finger.

'Goo-goo,' he said, excitedly pointing at

the screen.

'Yes, I agree, but you've still got to stay put,' she said.

Kitty sprawled in her usual position, and lost herself in the cartoon. Tom watched her, and suddenly he didn't like being left behind with nobody to hold him and pay him attention. He made some noises, but Kitty took no notice. She'd heard enough from her baby brother for one day.

Tom let himself fall to one side, then

rolled over on his tummy. He pulled himself up into the crawling position and moved along the sofa. All he wanted was to join Kitty, who had her back to him. But how was he to get down?

All Kitty heard was a thud, closely followed by another. She turned round and saw to her horror that Tom had fallen forward, right on his head, and flipped over, in a somersault, to land with a soft crash on the carpet. She was over by him in the time it took to think, Oh no!

He lay still.

Those seconds seemed to stretch into hours.

'Oh, Tom, please cry – *please.*'

All Kitty wanted was to hear that familiar sound, so she would know he was all right. He lay with his eyes closed, silent.

'MUUUUUUM!' she yelled.

'Hic – hic – WAAAAH-WAAAH-WAAAAH!' yelled Tom.

Mum came running in, to find both her children in tears. Looking scared she picked Tom up, but soon saw – and heard – that he was all right. Amidst much stammering and sobbing, Kitty told her what had happened.

'It – it-it w-w-w-as my f-f-fault,' she cried.

'No, love, shhhhh – it was an accident,' said Mum, in that soft soothing voice she used for the baby – who was crying as if he'd suddenly been given all the lungs of all the babies in the whole world.

Kitty snuggled up to them both, and soon Tom stopped screaming, because he saw her shaggy head and remembered how much fun it was to pull that hair. How Kitty enjoyed the pain! It made her laugh with relief.

Mum explained he'd been silent for those

few seconds just because he'd had a shock, and Kitty told her that she'd been so scared – not for herself, but for Tom.

'I'm always calling him a cry baby, but just now all that mattered was for him to yell again!' she said. 'Because then I'd know he was OK.'

'What else?'

'I just realised, *he*'s allowed to be a baby but' (she took a deep breath) 'I'm not – any more.'

'Oh, Kit,' said Mum. 'You know you'll always be my special baby girl! But listen, love – we all cry and we all get jealous and act like babies sometimes.'

'Even GUs?' said Kitty, her eyes open wide.

'Especially us!' said Mum.

chapter 5
No choice!

Rosie had been acting strangely but Kitty, Anita and William didn't really take any notice. Sometimes their friend could be moody, and they were used to letting her get over it in her own time. 'After all,' William said, 'Kitty, you can get in bad moods too, but me and Anita are always the same.'

'That means – sunny!' said Anita, looking as good as gold.

'But you and Rosie, Kit, you're cloudy types,' said William, with a big grin.

It was true.

Because of that they didn't really worry over Rosie, who wouldn't talk much and slouched off by herself at break time in a way that really was quite unusual. It was as if she was in a permanent sulk. When she had to go to see the head teacher, the children asked if she was in trouble, but she shook her head.

'She just wanted to talk to me,' she said. And nothing more.

Kitty decided that was very strange and thought something must be going on.

This continued for a few weeks. Then, one Friday, Kitty noticed a very old, very scruffy thin nylon roll-bag by Rosie's place in the cloakroom. It was a faded green and one end of the zip was held together with a safety pin. Rosie saw her looking at it, and kicked it further under the bench. Then she turned her back and walked off without saying anything.

Something's definitely wrong, Kitty thought.

Rosie was quieter than ever, and didn't speak to anyone at break. Normally the noisiest, jolliest girl in the class, it was as if a stranger had got into her body – a creature who looked stiff and sad, frightened and furious, all at the same time. In fact she looked just like Tough Tim had done when he joined the class, although he was better now since Kitty had challenged him.

Kitty couldn't bear it.

At dinner time she plucked up her courage – thinking, as she did so, that it was funny to have to be brave to talk to one of your friends.

'What's up, Rosie?' she asked.

'Nothing.'

'Come on, Rosie! Are we friends, or what?'

'Yes,' she said, very slowly, as if she wasn't sure.

'Well, talk to me!'

'What do you want me to say?' Rosie replied, looking miserable.

'Well, I could start by asking you why

you've brought that old bag to school, and you could try telling me.'

There was a long pause, then Rosie took a deep breath and said, 'It's got my stuff in it. I'm going to stay with my dad for the weekend.'

'Your dad?'

Now, Kitty knew that Rosie's dad lived at home with her mum and her brothers and sister. Kitty liked their house, because it was big and messy and full of fun, especially when Rosie's big brother played his guitar.

'Yes, he's moved out.'

'Moved out?'

Kitty felt silly. She knew she was just repeating what Rosie was saying, like an echo. But she was so shocked she didn't know what to say.

So – *that*'s what's wrong, she thought.

'Oh . . . I see . . . I'm sorry, Rosie.'

'Why?'

'Well – because, it can't be very nice for you.'

Rosie turned to her with a hard, bright look in her eyes. 'So what?' she said. 'Plenty of people split up, don't they?'

'Oh, yes,' said Kitty.

'I don't care a bit! It'll mean I get two

lots of presents at birthday and Christmas. Dad already bought me a new top 'cos he feels guilty! Anyway, they've been arguing so much lately it's a relief.'

'Oh, yes,' said Kitty.

'Mum says it's better for people to live in separate houses and get on, than live under one roof and be unhappy. She's right, isn't she?'

'Oh, yes,' said Kitty, lost for words.

Rosie stood kicking at the wall with the heel of her trainer. Kitty chewed her nail. The other children laughed and shouted and chased each other about. Their noise seemed very far away.

'So that's it, then,' Rosie said at last. 'I haven't been to his new place before. It's a little flat, and I'm staying tonight and the others are visiting tomorrow. Could be exciting.'

'Oh, yes,' Kitty said.

★ ★ ★

All weekend she thought about Rosie and wondered how she was getting on. There were other children in the class whose mums and dads didn't live together any more, so that didn't seem strange to Kitty. All she wanted was for Rosie to be happy, and for everything to work out for the best.

On Monday her friend seemed more cheerful. She told Kitty, William and Anita that she'd had a good time, even though Dad's flat was a bit small. On Saturday night she'd gone home to their mum with her big sister, and their brothers had stayed the night in turn.

'I suppose we'll all get used to it,' Rosie said, as if she was determined to. 'No choice really!'

Kitty really admired her attitude.

On Wednesday night Melissa had to come home for tea, because her mum couldn't collect her. Melissa still got on Kitty's nerves, even though she'd changed

for the better. It was just a habit really. Kitty guessed maybe she'd be *born* feeling irritated with her cousin, and that was just to do with families. You couldn't do anything about it. You were stuck with them.

No choice really – which was just what

Rosie had said.

The thing that annoyed her about Melissa was that, apart from being really pretty she was spoilt. She always had the best of everything: more presents and the most expensive clothes. And when the cousins were really small she never wanted to share anything, which Kitty thought was really mean – even though she didn't either!

They were messing about in Kitty's bedroom when something made Kitty tell Melissa about Rosie. She wasn't sure if she should, because it wasn't always right to talk about people.

'I wouldn't like that,' said Melissa slowly.

'Nor would I,' said Kitty.

'I think Tim's parents are divorced,' said Melissa.

'Really?'

'Yes. And I suppose you get used to it.'

'No choice!' said Kitty brightly.

So what!

The cousins felt close for once. They talked about all sorts of things, like families and friends and being jealous and not wanting to grow up, yet wanting to at the same time. After a while the conversation came back to Rosie.

'The thing is,' Kitty explained, 'when I saw that rotten bag by her peg I wondered what she was doing. Rosie likes nice things, and it must make it worse having to use that old thing.'

'Definitely!' Melissa said. 'When I came

to your school I thought Rosie was really cool.'

'She is!' smiled Kitty. 'But that bag isn't!'

At that moment, she thought she saw a gleam in Melissa's eye, but forgot about it.

Next morning Melissa arrived at school carrying a big plastic carrier. A group of the children were standing around in the cloakroom, when she asked, 'Does anybody need a bag?'

'What sort of bag?' asked Kitty.

'This thing.'

When Melissa revealed what was in the plastic carrier Kitty gaped. All folded up was the neatest, coolest sports bag, in purple, with a flash on the side, and pockets each end. She knew Melissa had been given it as one of her birthday presents and Kitty had wished it was hers. But she also knew Melissa liked it very much indeed. 'I'll have it!' came a chorus as the children crowded round.

Suddenly Kitty realised what Melissa was doing. 'Why don't *you* have it, Rosie,' she said brightly.

'It's brilliant, but why don't you want it?' asked Rosie, looking longingly at the sports bag.

'Oh, Mum's bought me a new one, so I'm spoilt for choice,' Melissa replied, in her most I-couldn't-care-less-because-I've-got-everything voice.

Kitty knew that wasn't true. She saw one or two of the others roll their eyes, and make faces at each other, thinking it just wasn't fair. But Kitty said nothing.

'Well . . .' said Rosie.

Kitty encouraged her. 'Go on, Rosie, you have it!'

'No, give it to me,' somebody called out.

'Oh, I think the colour suits Rosie,'

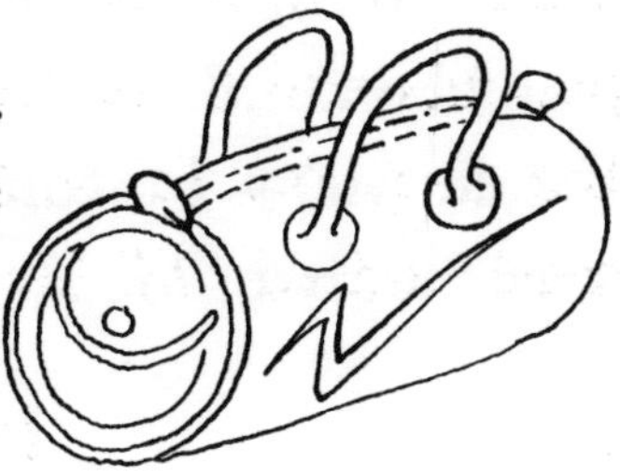

Melissa said carelessly. 'You like purple, don't you? There you are – take it off my hands so I've got some space in my cupboard.'

With that, she just thrust the bag into Rosie's arms, and sauntered casually out of the cloakroom before Rosie could even say thank you.

'Wow!' said Rosie, holding up the bag and examining it. 'This is mega-cool! Wait till I show Dad tomorrow!'

As the day went on, Kitty glanced at her cousin from time to time, seeing her in a new light. This was more important than new clothes or a new hairstyle. This really did seem like a new Melissa. And Kitty liked what she saw.

At last she found the moment to get her on her own, to tell her how brilliant that plan had been.

'But, Mel – I mean – I know you really *loved* that bag, so . . .'

So what!

'So what? I don't *need* it,' her cousin said, with a shrug.

'Won't your mum be cross you gave it away?' asked Kitty.

'Oh that's all right,' Melissa said. 'We'll just tell her I had no choice, eh Kit?'

Then Kitty linked her cousin's arm. 'Yes but, Melissa, what's really great is – you did!'

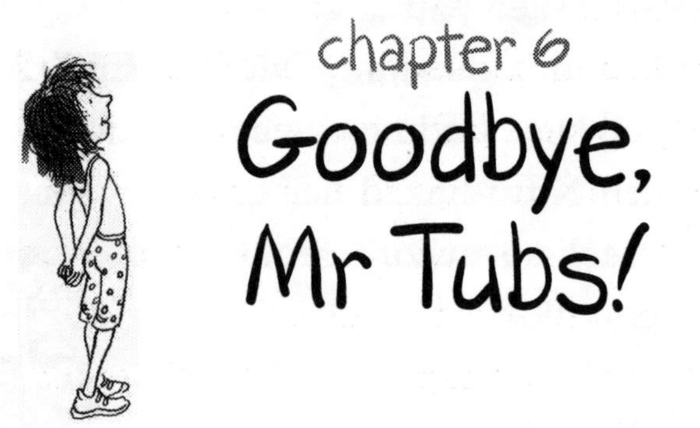

chapter 6

Goodbye, Mr Tubs!

Sometimes Kitty wondered if she was too old for Mr Tubs. She knew that was silly, because she loved her teddy so much. When he fell on the floor and lay there looking silly and uncomfortable with his head down and his bottom in the air, it made her so sad she just had to pick him up to save his feelings.

But in her heart she knew a teddy bear can't have feelings.

Can he?

Anyway, it was summertime, and Kitty's family were going on their first proper holiday for quite a while. Kitty was thrilled: a package holiday to Spain! She spent ages deciding what to take, and Mum made long lists. It was a cold rainy summer, as usual, and so they were all looking forward to the sun.

'Think of sitting in a deckchair all day!' said Dad.

'Getting a bit of a suntan!' said Mum.

'Swimming in warm water!' said Daniel.

'Playing beach games,' said Kitty.

Tom was asleep and didn't seem too bothered.

Kitty piled up on her bed all the clothes she thought she needed. Mum came in and told her to take half that amount.

'You've got to carry your own case, mind!' she warned.

'But what about all my felt-tips and

books and games?' she protested.

'You won't need them,' Mum said. 'You'll be on the beach all day, love, so just take as little as possible.'

The night before the holiday Kitty looked at her case, then at Mr Tubs.

'There's no room for you, you know,' she told him.

He looked at her with his big brown eyes.

'I'd really like you to come, Mr Tubs, but

you have to look after the house,' she whispered.

His paws were floppy. The bedroom light glinted on his sad eyes. His old ears seemed to droop. He seemed to be telling her she was silly, because he was too old and too squashy to look after anything.

Except Kitty.

And he'd always looked after Kitty, ever since Mum and Dad had given him to her on her first birthday. Mr Tubs was part of her life.

'It's no good,' she told him sternly. 'I'm not a little kid any more. I can't take a teddy on holiday, and anyway, look at my bag! You're too fat to fit in.'

At that he looked more miserable than ever.

Next morning they had to leave very very early to catch the bus for the airport. Because she was so excited, Kitty had a funny feeling in her tummy, as if she hadn't eaten or slept for a long time.

She pulled on her jeans, tee-shirt and zipped sweat top, and rushed to clean her teeth before Daniel got in the bathroom. Then she came back, with her new toilet bag patterned with fish, and put it on top of her packing.

She was about to zip the bag up when she felt eyes looking at her. She was sure Mr Tubs had been under her duvet, but now he seemed to have worked his way up to the top of her bed and lay looking at her mournfully from the pillow. Kitty couldn't stand it.

Quickly she pulled out some clothes and started to squash Mr Tubs into her bag. It was very hard and she was afraid the zip would break but at last Mr Tubs was packed. She was ready.

The journey to Spain seemed to take forever. The plane was late, and their luggage took ages to arrive in the baggage hall, and then there was another coach journey, so it was very late when they reached their hotel.

Mum and Dad shared a room with Baby Tom; Kitty and Daniel were next door. They were all pleased when they realised their rooms had a view of the promenade and the sea. Kitty squealed with delight at the necklace of lights spread out before them, and the scent of the warm air.

But now it was time to sleep. Kitty opened her bag to find her pyjamas, and when Mr Tubs tumbled out (he looked awfully hot in there!) Daniel pointed and laughed. 'You didn't bring Mr Tubs! Fancy taking your cuddly toy on holiday at your age!'

'So what? You're just stupid!' said Kitty, embarrassed. She jumped into bed with Mr Tubs in her arms – and slept.

But she was a little bit ashamed of her bear, and decided she wouldn't ever take him out of the room.

The next two weeks were the best ever, Kitty thought. There was something for all of them. Mum and Dad made friends with some other GUs, and there was a crèche run by two lovely German girls, where Mum could sometimes leave Baby Tom so she could have some free time.

Every day they went to the beach and swam and sunbathed. Mum made too much fuss about covering them with suncream all the time, but apart from that it was perfect. Kitty and Daniel played beach football and rounders with the other children on the tour.

Kitty and the rest of the family – except Tom – liked tasting new kinds of food. At night they

listened to local music, and danced at the disco. They went shopping for souvenirs, and Dad made them laugh by choosing a silly straw hat. Kitty bought little china donkeys with 'A Present From Spain' written on their backs, for Rosie, William and Anita. A few days later, she thought carefully and spent her last money on a necklace of tiny pink shells for Melissa.

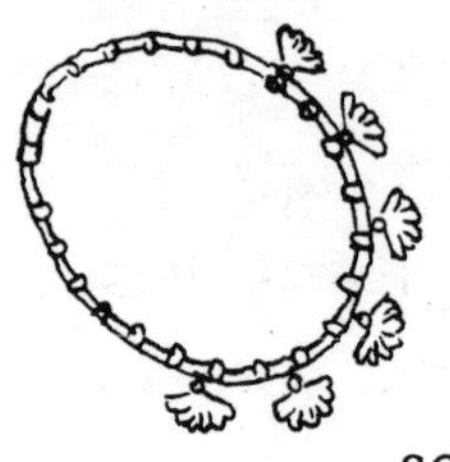

One of the nicest things about the holiday was Maria. She was the lady who looked after the rooms, and Kitty saw her most days. She had sparkling dark eyes above a wide smile that never seemed to disappear. Kitty asked her to teach her some words in Spanish – how to say 'please' and 'thank you'.

'*Por favor,*' Kitty said, proud of her new knowledge, and '*Gracias*! Is that right, Maria?'

'*Si, si!* – yes! And now, Keety, you say "*Verdadermente yo te quiera, Maria*!"'

Trying very hard, Kitty did her best to copy the sentence, then asked what it meant.

'You ees say to me – I really like you, Maria!' said Maria. She hugged Kitty and told her she was just like her own little girl.

Mr Tubs watched all this. He stayed in the room all day, looking after things, and Maria told Kitty that 'the handsome bear' had become her friend. Kitty was sure his mouth turned up at the corners at that!

'Does he talk to you, Maria?' she asked.

'*Naturalmente* – of course,' she replied.

'What does he say?'

'He tell me many secrets – and when I go he say "*Adios, Maria*".'

'But – he doesn't speak Spanish, does he?'

'Zees bear – he so clever he talk in all language!' Maria laughed.

Kitty was sure Spanish time was much faster than home time. It had to be, because their holiday drew to a close when it had only just started. They all dreaded the long journey back, which was made worse by the fact that this time they had to leave very late at night.

It was sad to say '*Adios*' to Maria and the other people in the hotel, and Kitty felt very cross and tired. She quarrelled with Daniel because she was sure he'd deliberately hidden her souvenirs, but he said she'd made the room such a mess no wonder everything got lost.

Mum told Kitty to hurry up or else they'd miss the coach. Dan yelled at her because she'd borrowed his pen to write postcards and lost it, and Dad said that was a waste of time because she'd been too lazy to finish writing them anyway. Then Mum and Dad got angry with each other over nothing much, and Baby Tom cried a lot. It was all because the holiday was over.

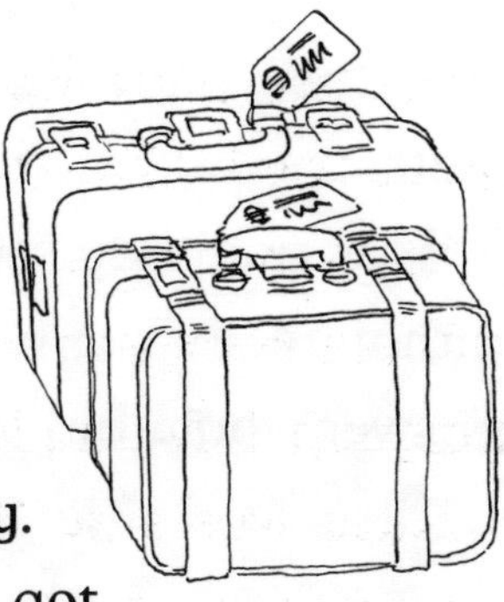

Travelling home seemed even longer and more boring than the journey there, but a part of Kitty began to feel pleased – looking forward to seeing her own room and her friends again. It's like that with holidays, she thought – you have a good time with what's new, but you realise how much you like your old things too.

Unpacking is horrible, but Mum soon bundled up all their dirty clothes and started loading the washing-machine. It was then that Kitty realised the terrible truth.

'Has anybody seen Mr Tubs?' she asked, although in her heart she knew what the answer would be.

There was no Mr Tubs in the whole house.

Mr Tubs had been forgotten . . . No. Kitty had left Mr Tubs behind. It was her own fault and nobody else's.

So what!

'Oh, Kitty,' said Mum, meeting her eyes, and kneeling down to hug her.

'I told you you were stupid to take him!' said Daniel.

'I'll telephone the hotel,' said Dad. 'They're bound to have found him.'

But the truth is, the hotel was very big and was already full of new package holiday-makers. The girl on the reception desk didn't speak very good English and she didn't care very much either. She told Dad, sorry, no toy had been handed in. So that was that.

Kitty wanted to howl her heart out, but she saw her family watching her and decided she couldn't.

'I don't *really* mind,' she said with a shrug.

'Good girl,' smiled Dad, patting her on the shoulder.

'Maybe I was getting too old for that bear anyway,' she said.

'That's a really grown-up attitude,

Kitsy,' said Mum, giving her a kiss.

Then they went on unpacking and looking after the baby as if nothing had happened.

Daniel just looked at her closely, then went upstairs to his room. Kitty expected him to crow, and was surprised that he'd said nothing. She knew she had to hide quickly before she burst into tears.

When she closed the door to her room, she flung herself on the bed and cried and cried. It was so awful to think of Mr Tubs sitting there on his own, probably covered by the bedclothes in that mess of a room. Or – worse – on the floor under the bed. She wondered when he'd realised he'd been left behind. Forgotten . . . and with nobody even saying goodbye to him . . .

Of course teddy bears have feelings!

The thought made Kitty cry all the more. It was too terrible to realise she'd never again cuddle that familiar fur which

smelt so sweetly of hugs. She cuddled her pillow and murmured, '*Adios*, Mr Tubs.'

After a while she heard a knock on her door. She jumped up and opened it. Daniel was standing on the landing with his hands behind his back.

'Er . . . I wondered if you'd like some company,' he said, coming into her room. 'Bibi said he'd quite like to spend some time with you.'

Then, to Kitty's amazement he held out his favourite old toy, the one she hadn't seen for a long time. Bibi was a shapeless creature, a cross between a rabbit, a koala

bear and a grey squirrel. Nobody knew what he was supposed to be – this floppy home-made toy Mum had bought in a church craft sale before Kitty was born. Of course, Daniel had always loved him more than his expensive soft toys, and at one time Bibi had gone with him everywhere.

'I d-d-didn't know you still had him,' Kitty sniffed.

'Oh, I'll always keep Bibi! He lives in a box in my cupboard I made as – er – as a sort of nest for him. And shall I tell you a secret, Kit?'

She nodded.

'When I'm feeling very fed up or scared – like the night before I went to big school, or when I had to go to have my tooth out – I get him out and cuddle him.'

'Still?' blinked Kitty.

'Not very often – but, yes.'

'But I thought . . .'

'So what! Lots of people keep their toys till they're grown up, Kitty. What's wrong with that? It's nothing to be ashamed of – whatever I said.'

'I want Mr Tubs,' said Kitty, her eyes starting to fill with tears again.

'I know you do,' said her brother quickly. 'That's why I thought you might like to borrow Bibi until . . . well, until you've got used to not having Mr T, Bibi said he'd really like to have a holiday in your room, didn't you, squirrel-face?'

He looked down at the old toy and grasped the back of its neck to make it nod. Bibi was so short of stuffing his head waggled up and down and looked very funny. Kitty smiled, then laughed.

She took Bibi and put him on her pillow. It would be untrue to say it was just as good as having Mr Tubs to cuddle, because it wasn't. But that night, and for the next week, funny old Bibi helped her sleep and almost forget the fact that she'd carelessly deserted her beloved bear.

Then, one Saturday morning just before the new school term began, they were all downstairs when the doorbell rang. 'I'll answer it!' said Kitty.

So what!

The postman was holding a large, bulky parcel, done up with lots of tape. 'Somebody's got a present today!' he said cheerfully. 'From abroad, by the looks of it.'

Kitty couldn't believe it. The name on the package – written in bold black ink – was hers. Something started to flutter inside her chest – that feeling you have when something really wonderful is going to happen, as if there's a whole flock of butterflies dancing from flower to flower with the joy of the spring.

She raced into the kitchen, and waved it over her head. 'I think I've got . . . I think they've . . . Ohh, Danny, help me open this!'

It didn't take long before the brown paper was off – and a rather squashed-looking Mr Tubs was smiling up at them from the breakfast table.

'Well, just look!' smiled Dad.

'Ook . . . be-be-be-be-be,' gurgled Baby Tom, looking delighted.

'But who could've done this?' wondered Mum. 'How strange there's no letter.'

'I bet I can guess!' laughed Daniel.

Kitty didn't say anything of course, because she was clutching her teddy and burying her face in his head. She didn't have any words to describe how she felt.

'Look, there's a label round his neck,' Daniel cried out.

They all examined the large cream cardboard label, tied neatly round the bear's neck with a red ribbon. The carefully printed black letters said:

'*POR FAVOR CUIDA DE ESTE AGRADABLE VIEJO OSO*'

'What does that mean, Dad?' Kitty asked.

Dad frowned as he tried to remember the little Spanish he knew. At last he said, 'I know! It says – please take care of this, er . . . agreeable old bear.'

'Handsome,' said Kitty.

'What?'

'Handsome – Maria always called him that. I know it's Maria who's sent him home.'

'She must have got our address from the hotel – how kind,' murmured Mum.

'Maria was lovely,' whispered Kitty, and when she looked into Mr Tubs' eyes she knew he agreed.

You can imagine how Kitty felt! It was like all the Christmases and birthdays she'd ever known rolled into one. She felt that she could never be as happy as this again in her whole life – so happy she wanted to dance.

So she waltzed upstairs with Mr Tubs, and introduced him to Bibi. Then, very carefully, she took the shapeless old toy through into Daniel's room and laid him gently on her brother's pillow. 'Thanks, Bibi,' she whispered.

That night when she went to bed, she hugged Mr Tubs as if she would never let him go again, and told him she was sorry she'd said it didn't matter that he was left behind.

'I didn't mean it, Mr Tubs – you see, I was just trying to be big 'n' brave,' she said. 'But you know I won't ever be too big for you, and I'll love you for ever. Isn't that right, old bear?'

And she was sure – absolutely sure – Mr Tubs said, '*Si*!'